MEET ALL THESE FRIENDS IN BUZZ BOOKS:

Thomas the Tank Engine
The Animals of Farthing Wood
Biker Mice From Mars
James Bond Junior
Fireman Sam
Joshua Jones
Rupert
Babar

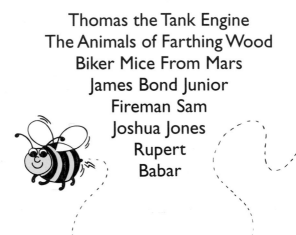

First published in Great Britain 1994 by Buzz Books,
an imprint of Reed Children's Books
Michelin House, 81 Fulham Road, London SW3 6RB
and Auckland, Melbourne, Singapore and Toronto

ISBN 1 85591 391 7

Printed in Italy by Olivotto

Unwelcome Visitors

Story by Colin Dann
Text by Mary Risk
Illustrations by The County Studio

Spring was slow in coming to White Deer Park. For the Farthing Wood animals, winter had meant cold and hunger. They all longed for the warmth of spring.

One morning, Vole was found dead.

"He lived to a good age," said Fox.

But he and all his friends were sad.

Owl brought more bad news.

"The warden is gone," she said. "I saw two men carry him out of his cottage and put him into a white van. He looked very ill."

"Oh dear," said Badger. "I hope he's all right. I wonder who will look after Cat?"

"I saw a woman take her away in a basket," said Owl. "I wouldn't waste your sympathy on Cat."

Only Mole was well and happy. It was warmer underground than above in the snow, and the worms were plentiful.

Someone else was underground too.

"Hello? Anyone at home?" said a voice one day, and a furry little female dropped into Mole's tunnel.

"Oh! I say! Hello!" said Mole in delight.

But a new danger was coming to White Deer Park. One night Whistler heard a loud bang that echoed in the still night air.

"A gun!" he said fearfully. "Like the one that made a hole in my wing!"

"Kee!" called Kestrel in alarm. "A deer has been shot!"

Fox frowned at the news. "The deer will need our help," he said. "We must be alert, and warn Stag if the poachers return."

The poachers did come back that night. They moved quietly, but Fox's keen ears heard them.

"I'll go and warn Stag," he whispered to Vixen. "Tell the others!"

Stag stood with his herd, his proud head raised. The man lifted his gun and took aim.

Quickly, Fox barked a warning to his friend.

Stag dodged out of the way, while the rest of the herd scattered. But one doe was too slow. She fell to the ground, dead.

Fox looked at the doe lying in the snow.

"We must stop the poachers," he said.

"All you can do is warn us," replied Stag gravely. "Then we must take our chance."

"Maybe, but I've got an idea," said Fox.

12

The leader of the blue foxes heard everything. Scarface didn't like the poachers, but he hated Fox even more.

"So Fox thinks he's cleverer than all of us!" he thought jealously.

The next day, he pounced on Weasel.

"Help! Let me go!" squealed Weasel.

"Have you forgotten our agreement?" he snarled. "You promised to spy on Fox, but you haven't told me anything yet."

"S-sorry, Mr Scarface," gulped Weasel.

Spring was on its way at last. As the thaw settled in, icicles fell from the trees and the snow began to melt.

"Here's a lovely big worm for you," said Mole to his new friend, Mateless.

"It's almost time to think about nests," Speedy told Whistler.

Fox was busy making plans. He trotted about in the melting snow, and watched Kestrel play at the edge of the pond where the ice was shrinking away from the bank.

Beside him, Vixen was worried. "We've not seen Weasel for weeks," she said.

"I'm sure she'll turn up," Fox replied.

Weasel was miserable.

"I can't spy on Fox!" she thought. "He can be an old bossy boots sometimes, but he's still my friend. I'll just have to keep away from the other Farthing Wood animals, then I won't have anything to tell Scarface."

But Scarface tracked her down.

"I don't know!" squealed Weasel.

"Don't know what?" said Scarface. "I haven't asked you anything yet."

"But I don't know anything!" insisted Weasel. "Honest!"

Later, Kestrel saw something strange.

"A moving gorse bush?" she thought.
"That's odd."

"Ouch! Nasty old thorns!" wailed Weasel.

"Weasel! What are you doing?" said
Kestrel, flying down to investigate.

"I'm not Weasel, I'm a gorse bush," said
Weasel. "Don't talk to me! Don't tell me
anything! Leave me alone!"

That evening Fox sent everyone to their posts. Kestrel and Owl kept watch from above. Whistler patrolled the park's boundary. Hare, whose sensitive body could feel far-off vibrations, listened for the tread of approaching feet.

Stag and his herd pawed the ground restlessly, afraid of the coming attack.

"They're here! The poachers are coming!" gasped Hare. "I feel their footsteps."

Kestrel followed the poachers, while Owl
flew like the wind to Fox's earth.

"They appear to be here," she said.

Fox sped away at once towards the pond.

"The poachers are coming!" he called to Stag. "I'll lure them the other way."

He ran on through the wood.

"Hurry, Fox! They're moving fast!" chattered Squirrel from a tree branch.

"Thanks!" gasped Fox. "Keep watching."

"Fox! They're moving away!" called Kestrel from above.

Fox lifted his head high, and gave a screaming bark.

"It's that fox again," said a poacher. "He scared the deer away last time. Let's shoot him first."

Their heavy feet crashed through the wood as they followed Fox's scream.

The poachers were nearly at the pond. They could see the deer, but no Fox. Stag watched, nervously standing his ground.

"Keep still!" hooted Owl to the rest of the animals.

They hid nearby, watching and waiting.

"Fox! They're pointing the guns at Stag! Go now!" shouted Vixen suddenly.

Fox barked again and ran out from the bushes to stand in front of Stag. The moon had risen and the poachers could see Fox clearly now.

"Get that fox!" shouted one of them.

But Fox was too quick. He ran into the bushes, then back out amongst the deer.

The poachers couldn't keep track of him.

Fox slid beneath the herd of deer and onto the icy pond. It creaked under his weight.

"There he is! After him!" called the men.

Fox reached the other side of the frozen pond, and scrambled up the bank to safety.

The men didn't notice that the ice on the pond was melting. Wild with anger, they ran onto the pond after Fox.

24

The ice cracked. With a roar of fear and
rage, one of the poachers fell into the
freezing water. The other dropped his gun,
and put out a hand to help him. But the ice
was too slippery. He fell in too, and both
guns sank to the bottom of the pond.

Dripping and cursing, the poachers left the
park empty-handed.

The Farthing Wood animals and their friends, the deer, crowded round Fox to congratulate him on his brilliant plan.

Scarface watched the celebrations from a nearby ridge.

"So now Fox is a hero," he said to his mate. "We'll see about that."

"Dear me! What's that?" said Badger, pointing to a log which seemed to be cheering loudly. He tipped it over with his paw. "It's Weasel! Where have you been?"

"Me? Nowhere! I haven't done anything! I haven't said a word!" cackled Weasel nervously. And she scampered off.

When the celebrations had finished, Fox and Vixen returned to their earth.

"I wonder what Weasel is up to," said Fox.

"I don't know," smiled Vixen. "But we've got other things to think about. Fox, you're going to be a father!"